THE LITTLE RED LIGHTHOUSE
and
THE GREAT GRAY BRIDGE

THE LITTLE RED LIGHTHOUSE

and

THE GREAT GRAY BRIDGE

by HILDEGARDE H. SWIFT
and LYND WARD

HARCOURT, INC.
San Diego New York London

Once upon a time a little lighthouse was built on a sharp point of the shore by the Hudson River.

It was round and fat and red.

It was fat and red and jolly.

And it was VERY, VERY PROUD.

Behind it lay New York City where the people lived.

Before it sailed the boats on which the people rode. Up and down, up and down, sailed the boats. On and on and on rolled the river. All the way from Lake Tear-in-the-clouds, high up in the mountains, came the Hudson River. It rolled down the mountains. It rolled and rolled and rolled. It rolled past Albany. It rolled past New York. And it went on forever looking for the sea.

Now the boats on the river talked to the little red lighthouse as they passed,

"Hoot, hoot, hoot! How are you?" said the big steamer, with its deep, throaty whistle.

"SSSSSSSSalute!" lisped the slender canoe as it slid along the shore.

"Chug, chug, chug, ch-ch-ch-cheerio!" called the fat, black tug as it puffed on its way, pulling a load of coal on a barge.

By day the little red lighthouse did not answer.

It was quiet when the boats called.

It was still.

But every night, just at fall of dark, a man came to tend the little red lighthouse. He took out his jingling keys. He unlocked the small red door in its side. He climbed its steep and winding stairs, up, up, up, to the very top. He took off the thick white cap that let it sleep by day. He turned on the gas with a funny small black key.

Up, up, up, flowed the gas from the six red tanks below.

Then the little red lighthouse spoke out plainly.

Flash! Flash! Flash!

One second on, two seconds off! Look out! Watch me! Danger, danger, danger!

Watch my rocks! Keep away!

FLASH! FLASH! FLASH!

It felt big and useful and important. What would the boats do without me? it thought.

It felt VERY, VERY PROUD.

The boats saw the light and were safe. The boats saw it, and they kept to the channel. The boats were grateful to the little red lighthouse.

Sometimes a fog crept up the river. Then the man came to wind up a big black clock inside the little red lighthouse. He wound and wound and wound it. The clock was joined to an iron bell outside.

The bell began to ring.

Warn-ing! Warn-ing! it said.

Flash! said the light.

Warn-ing! said the bell.

The little red lighthouse had two voices then.

Every day it felt bigger and prouder.

Why, I am MASTER OF THE RIVER, it thought.

Then one day a gang of workmen came and began to dig.

They dug and dug and dug.

By and by great steel girders began to rise up against the sky.

A big group of men were carried over the Hudson on a barge. Across the barge stood four great reels, and from each reel there trailed a slender silver line.

All the boats on the river stopped moving.

All the near-by boats turned to look.

Even the river seemed to be very, very still.

When the men came back, they seemed happy.

"The first cables are over," they called. "The catwalk will be up soon." And the other men shouted "Hurrah!"

What do they mean? thought the little red lighthouse.

What are these things called cables that are over?

Now the days and weeks went by. Every night the little lighthouse spoke plainly.

Flash! Flash! Flash!

Every day it watched the strange new gray thing beside it grow and grow. Huge towers seemed to touch the sky. Strong loops of steel swept across the river.

How big it was!

How wonderful!

How powerful!

A great gray bridge, spanning the Hudson River from shore to shore. It made the little red lighthouse feel very, very small.

Then one night a great beam of light flashed from the top of the nearest gray tower.

Flash! Turn! Flash!

Now I am needed no longer, thought the little red lighthouse. My light is so little and this one so big!

Perhaps they will give me up.

Perhaps they will tear me down.

Perhaps they will forget to turn my light on!

That night it stood waiting and waiting.

It felt glum and anxious and queer.

The night grew darker and darker.

Why did the man not come?

The little red lighthouse could neither speak nor shine.

Then in the middle of the night there came a storm. The wind moaned. The waves beat against the shore.

A thick fog crept over the river and tried to clutch the boats one by one.

The fat black tug was just coming back from Albany. It was caught and blinded by the fog. It looked for the little red lighthouse, but it could not find it. It listened for the bell, but it could not hear it. So thick the fog was, it could not see the light flashing high up from the great gray bridge.

CRASH! CRASH! CRASH!

The fat black tug ran upon the rocks and lay wrecked and broken.

Then the great gray bridge called to the little red lighthouse:

"Little brother, where is your light?"

"Am I brother of yours, bridge?" wondered the lighthouse. "Your light was so bright that I thought mine was needed no more."

"I call to the airplanes," cried the bridge. "I flash to the ships of the air. But you are still master of the river. Quick, let your light shine again. Each to his own place, little brother!"

So the little red lighthouse tried to shine once more, but though it tried and tried and tried, it could not turn itself on.

This is the end of me, it thought.

This is really the end.

My man will not come. I cannot turn myself on. Very likely I shall never shine again.

Dark and silent it stood.

And it was VERY, VERY SAD.

But at last it heard the door opening far below. At last it heard steps rushing up the stairs.

Why, here was the man hurrying to tend it.

"Where have you been, man? I thought you were never coming?"

"Oh, those boys! Those boys! They stole my keys! This will never happen again!"

Now the little red lighthouse knew that it was needed.

The bridge wanted it.

The man wanted it.

The ships must need it still.

It sent a long, bright, flashing ray out into the night.

One second on, two seconds off!

Flash, flash, flash!

Look out! Danger! Watch me! it called.

Soon its bell was booming out too.

Warn-ing! Warn-ing! it cried.

The little red lighthouse still had work to do. And it was glad.

And now beside the great beacon of the bridge the small beam of the lighthouse still flashes.

Beside the towering gray bridge the lighthouse still bravely stands. Though it knows now that it is little, it is still VERY, VERY PROUD.

And every day the people who go up Riverside Drive in New York City turn to look at it. For there they both are—the great gray bridge and the little red lighthouse.

If you don't believe it, go see for yourselves!

www.HarcourtBooks.com

Library of Congress Cataloging-in-Publication Data
Swift, Hildegarde Hoyt.
The little red lighthouse and the great gray bridge/
Hildegarde H. Swift; illustrated by Lynd Ward.
p. cm.
Summary: A little lighthouse on the Hudson River regains its pride when it finds out that it is still useful and has an important job to do.
[1. Lighthouses—Fiction.]
I. Ward, Lynd, 1905–, ill. II. Title.
PZ7.S978Li 2002
[E]—dc21 2001007106
ISBN 0-15-204571-6

TWP 9 11 13 15 16 14 12 10
4500217521

PRINTED IN SINGAPORE

Photography of original art by Gamma One, New York, New York
The display type was set in Frys Baskerville and the text type was set in Berthold Baskerville by R&S Book Composition, La Mesa, California.
Color separations by Colourscan Co. Pte. Ltd., Singapore
Printed and bound by Tien Wah Press, Singapore
This book was printed on 104 gsm Cougar Opaque Natural Woodfree paper.
Production supervision by Sandra Grebenar and Pascha Gerlinger

A NOTE ABOUT THE FACSIMILE EDITION

Hildegarde H. Swift's story was inspired by her reaction to seeing the George Washington Bridge when it was first being built, just as it began to overshadow the little lighthouse below. This enhanced facsimile edition re-creates the experience of reading the story as it was first published in 1942. The type has been reset–certain letters and punctuation were digitally crafted–and the cream-colored paper is used once again, bringing the original warmth back to each page. Printing materials for the first edition could not be found, but the search for them led to a thrilling discovery: Lynd Ward's original watercolors for the story.

Lynd Ward sat on the Manhattan bank of the Hudson River and sketched the lighthouse and the bridge. Because they were under military guard following the 1941 attack on Pearl Harbor, Ward worked furiously as his wife, author May McNeer, served as a lookout. Later, using his on-site pencil sketches of the lighthouse, bridge, and shoreline as a reference, Ward rendered the scenes in black ink, then added red and blue watercolors. No one knew that he had painted these images, however, because Ward created three-color artwork based on the watercolors for the original book. The artwork was identical to the watercolors in form but lacked their nuances and luminosity.

The original watercolors now appear in this edition, uniting, for the first time, Lynd Ward's original vision for the book with the classic text by Hildegarde H. Swift that inspired him.

The Little Red Lighthouse and the Great Gray Bridge *is also available as a smaller gift edition that is part of a Lullaby Lights night-light set.*